Peterio and The Astronomy Project

Acknowledgements

I also thank Aaron from Advance Printers for the manuscript editing and layout.

Cover photo: Greenstein, G. (2013). The Andromeda Galaxy. Understanding the Universe.

Peterio and the Astronomy Project is a sequel to **Peterio Ignitus Planetary Anthropologist**

Table of Contents   Page

Chapter 1   Way to Go!

Peterio excitedly logs into his journal, Interplanetary Studies, to start a new study of his upcoming astronomy project.   It has come to pass for him to step whole heartedly into the vitalisation of radio astronomy beyond Earth.

The headquarters for astronomy is Earth.   Evidence for the origins of the Universe, its composition and continual evolution over the eons is used by the scientists who devise theories in the study of astronomy.   A model of a dynamic universe is continuously being built.

On Earth data amassed from observatories located at human colonised planets in the Milky Way Galaxy or from travelling space telescopes is being utilised in the mapping of the Milky Way Galaxy.   Human colonisation throughout this galaxy enabled the discovery of extra-Human life in planets nearby.   This research was key to the modelling of the presence and origins of life in the Universe.

For Peterio, the resurgence of study into astronomy is

an exciting anticipation, as he now has explored the Milky Way Galaxy. Moreover, he recently reached out to other galaxies, such as the Andromeda Galaxy. In this new project, he is part of a plan to involve the colonists living on planets of the Andromeda Galaxy. It is the year 2500 AD, 400 years since Peterio left Earth, to be a space faring scientist.

Peterio writes into his journal,

Astronomical data is retrieved from all sources including space telescopes, those either on satellites or stationed at observatories on planets at the Milky Way Galaxy.

The huge cosmos is full of stars which burst into life after the Big Bang. This event led to the abundant production of hydrogen and helium. The fusion between these two elements are reactions essential to the production of more elements and star formation. Stars such as the main sequence stars, yellow stars, orange stars, and those like the Sun, were born. There are the dwarf stars, white dwarfs, red dwarfs, blue dwarfs and giant stars, in varying stages of luminosities, which had their birth in the epochs of stellar formation. A red giant may suddenly expand and then collapse into a neutron star. The supernova event or expansion of this type of star will shed elements which are the material necessary for planet formation.

It is not only about stars, however fascinating, but it is also about the planets which whirl around these stars. It may be more about the possibility of finding life on these planets. Seeking out star systems have inspired Humankind on Earth for thousands of years, much before space farers like myself set afoot from Earth to explore.

For these efforts into research, exploration and discovery; museums were built for the Astronomical Societies to house all their treasured and award-winning photos. Telescopic photos captured the infinite space and the stars which dot this vastness. There are images of galaxies shaped, spiral, elliptical or other shapeless forms. Some photos exposed the less obvious images of black holes or the colourful illuminations of the nebulae. These collections went on exhibition and had always delighted all those amateurs and professional astronomers alike. It is a time on the Earth when the Humans held an honoured place in the historical scheme of the Universe.

Peterio cannot refrain from reminiscing on his past, when he worked in Astronomy. In his youth, on many a camping expedition, Peterio with his friends went out at night, to look for the constellations in the dark skies. Inspired by all the constellations which he viewed both from the Northern and Southern

Hemisphere of the Earth, Peterio captured and projected his view of such panorama onto canvas. With sparkling paint to draw the stars, he was able to outline all the visible constellations which his friends were able to identify. Later, as a junior member of the Earth Space Agency, he learned to use telescopes to find exoplanets. Eventually, Peterio graduated from the astrophysics program at college and during his years at graduate studies, had mapped habitable exoplanets for several star systems in the Milky Way.

Peterio's lust and love for travel sent him on a visit to the space stations orbiting the Earth, when he was just in high school. His excitement to be a space traveller was revealed in his learning to pilot planes and space vehicles in his college years.

Presently, Peterio is extremely pleased about the current decision made by the Committee for Planetary Studies to start an astronomy project at the Andromeda Galaxy. It would enable him again to participate in the most heartfelt activities of his youth on Earth. Peterio, after a brief career in astronomy, had sidetracked his focus from the study of space, stars, and planets to the study of the Human species, Homo sapiens. This happened when he decided to become a space farer and leave Earth for a life in other planets during the 22nd Century AD.

Currently Peterio puts all his efforts into studies of anthropology, especially that of the Human colonies at the galaxies, Milky Way and Andromeda. As chief anthropologist, he brought back to Earth, his most peculiar but awesome find. These newly explored planets at the Andromeda Galaxy, which to everyone's surprise, are inhabited by the Archaic Humans, Neanderthals and Denisovans from prehistoric Earth.

It is a real eye opener for all who eventually heard about the contact established by Peterio with the Archaic Humans in these planets so far away. These Archaic Humans have been transported by Force, hundreds of thousands of years ago. As the Earthlings kept progressing on the Earth, the Archaic humans went on their own path of development in these far away planets. There had been no contact with others until their discovery by Peterio. Peterio explained to his scientific community that Force deliberately sent him to these early Humans.

Presently, the Archaic Humans at Denisovana have achieved sophistication through the helpful and dedicated work of the colonist, Alfred Mendel. Denisovana is populated with Denisovans now led by Tedrid, a native Denisovan, and other Humans who replaced Alfred when he died. Peterio admires them greatly for their interests to be regarded as an Archaic Human colony in the Human Colonisation Project.

Especially thrilling for Peterio is when he talks to Theodore, a native Neanderthal, who is designated the leader at Neanderthala. Theodore reveals much anticipation to be included like the Denisovans in the Human Colonisation Project. The Neanderthals achieve much on their own, being independent as they often are. Although, the Denisovans got much educational directive from Peterio's colleagues, the Neanderthals were mostly excluded from the influence of Human help.

The Neanderthals' advancements at Neanderthala bring them to a level comparable to the Homo sapiens living in the Medieval Age on Earth. By now, they have discovered the advantages of using fire, hunting tools and weapons. They brought these skills with them, here from their time living on Earth. Later with the ability to manipulate fire, they learned to forge metal into alloys to make more sophisticated tools and weapons.

The Neanderthals are not active in warfare with each other, but they are very challenged for their survival in the habitats at Neanderthala. It is a very uninhabited place, except for the few animals that evolved there. In the past, in looking for shelter away from attack by ferocious animals, these Neanderthals hid away from the open grassland savannas.   Rocks from the rock faces of the cliffs and mountains were collected for their use in their search for food and shelter. They found liveable space inside the cavernous spaces within these mountainous slopes. For thousands of years, they had lived in the same way that humans lived out their cave life on Earth. However, they met with a beastly animal species who survived in the caves also.   These wild animals resemble those members of the cat family on Earth. When caught they were eaten by these Neanderthals. It was also the opposite scenario as they in turn, were prey to these beasts. Eventually, threatening relations with the predators made the Neanderthals leave the caves.

To their surprise, they found that they can live, in the open plains.   Here were plentiful amounts of less vicious animals. The Neanderthals made a choice to hunt these ungulates who migrated throughout the plains. With the stalks of the plants and branches of the trees that they can find in these grasslands, they started to build simple structures to take shelter. They remained nomadic, moving from place to place and had not any sense for community yet. Over the thousands of years that passed, the Neanderthals learned farming and became able to grow their own food and a sense of social communication started. Still, they never kept any livestock, but continued in the hunt for animal food.

There is a separation of the different groups of the Neanderthals. Members of the different Neanderthal populations did communicate with one another. Together on this planet where the land is not too fertile, the different groups also became uniquely adapted to each peculiar surrounding. In a particular circumstance, some found water holes where they hunted. So that group of Neanderthals went after the water borne fish by wading and swimming in the waters, as they did on Earth. These Neanderthals survived on this planet with a simple life with little need to build sophisticated weaponry.

Peterio on several occasions, was sent by Force to give

some help to those Neanderthals, when they were trapped in situations.   Peterio was not told by Force what to do. In a flash of a moment, he knew he must help the Neanderthals, incapacitated as they were. Once, he saved the Ancient Humans from a predator prey set up, as a pack of the hunting beasts was about to pounce on a small group of them. It was a decision to disrupt this life and death situation when Peterio blasted at the beasts using his high energy laser weapon.   Peterio never much uses this weapon as he rarely is involved in a hunt. News of Peterio was circulated, each time he was there to help the Neanderthal get out of the desperate traps they were caught in.

Peterio, during each visit found ways to boost their entry into civilisation. Peterio used sign language to facilitate communication with these primitives, when he spoke to them in his own language, English. Peterio is multilingual and can express his fluency of speech, in many languages. With the Archaic humans he also, often expressed some words in their own style of communication. Their own language was primitive and lost on Earth, not being retained by those humans who intermarried with them.

In contrast, Human colonists were very supportive of formal education for the Denisovans, after what they have seen from their lives with Alfred. With the Neanderthals, they decided not to regulate the education, but let their inquisitiveness guide the course of action. After contacts were made with these Archaic beings, more communication and visits to Denisovana and Neanderthala were carried out. In this region of outer space, members of the Humankind were brought together from different times and spaces. Now the space age Humans and the prehistoric Neanderthals and Denisovans are in contact with each other in an event unexpected but historic.

Nearby these planets where the Archaic were found, the Human Space Age Colonists in the Andromeda Galaxy, lived out their own particular lives on several different planets. Each planetary population revealed some uniqueness from their planetary adaptations and from cultural peculiarities brought from Earth. These planetary populations kept up their visits with each other, and now they were more than delighted to include as colonists also, the ancestral Humans. Eager to learn about each other's ongoing in their own respective settlements, they were able to maintain a lively interplanetary visiting program.

As Peterio writes these stories into his log, he scratches his head. He wonders whether this new expansive radio astronomy program and the ever-growing project in interplanetary visits at the Andromeda Galaxy, will make history in the story of Human achievements.

Peterio considers that there will be education into astronomy, and the building on each planet of observatories equipped with computerised systems of radio telescopes, and different forms of antennas and radio receivers. After having studied the methods of radio astronomy, each newly ranked amateur astronomer will be able to interpret data from the radio waves received. All those professionally educated and amateur alike, will also have a chance to visually explore the space at the Andromeda Galaxy using all different kinds of telescopes.

Peterio knows that he will be recruiting scientists from Earth and the Milky Way colonies to set up the observatories at these far away planets in the Andromeda Galaxy. *"The time has come"* says Peterio*"to reach out"*. There had been only a few colonists who kept up with the astronomy club activities in the exploration of the night skies at Andromeda. Although, the colonists are not making any claims in research; and radio communication is used mostly to keep up the rapport with the Milky way astronomers. Until now, the concern at these planets had only been to establish successfully these new settlements and maintain longevity. *"And so far, so good"*Peterio chuckles.

Peterio has an adrenaline rush as his heart beat very fast while he is thinking about all this. Peterio is presently about to take on the objective to initiate a highly ranked astronomy project. At 550 years old, Peterio is the leader of many a space-oriented program and he continues to be happy and amazed in every endeavour he takes on.

For the record, in vitalising a radio astronomy program at the colonies, these scientists will be seeking from Andromeda Galaxy, new data about the vast stretch of space in this galaxy. The Universe is alive with stellar activity and would be available for the astronomers there to witness and study. This project is designated for all the Space Age colonists and these Archaic Humans. Humanity has been directed to be here presently to map this corner of the Universe and this participation is both vision and mission.

Any intelligent extra-Human signals, beacons from far away will be sought after also by all the astronomers alike.

Beyond their enthusiasm for their role as passengers in the interplanetary explorations, both Archaic Humans are pleased to be oriented scientifically now, with the space faring Homo sapiens.

Chapter 2   **Meet over Coffee**

Peterio and Andreus are close comrades in the exploration of planets and in the pursuit to locate and study planetary life at far away galaxies. The study of any planetary inhabitation is challenging and is a model for scientific study. Peterio's pioneering work with Andreus at the galaxies Andromeda and Triangulum, was not only respected by his scientific community but was personally rewarding.

These colonists are far away from their home in the Milky Way galaxy; thus, in their own independent way they have to be successful. Still, life can be wonderful and full of opportunities. Peterio met his wife and started a family at the Andromeda Galaxy. Indeed Peterio, although he goes back to Earth on special visits, is presently making a life out amongst the stars. And much to the surprise of all the space faring colonists, is their making friendship with the Archaic Humans.

But today, they will run a meeting on the astronomy project that will be based at the Andromeda galaxy. They are sitting with Tedrid, Theodore and Evala at this meeting that was most looked forward to. To be served with coffee, that is made with coffee beans derived from Earth, makes the meeting all the more refreshing. The aroma of coffee stirs through the air in this beautiful room which has a sky-light. The view reveals the darkness of the evening sky. Bright shining lights made visible the tops of trees whose branches of large leaves are swaying in the wind. Planet Drake X is the place where they will engage with ideas.

It is at the Science Agriculture Farm at Drake X, a colonist planet, where Peterio decides to meet. Overlooking various fields of plants which are part of crop breeding experiments, the visitors can see the many crops that are being perfected by the colonists. Peterio explains that coffee is cherished on Earth, but other types of plant beans are also selected from the wild native plants here. The aroma of beans from the roastery swirl in the night breeze throughout. The newcomers Tedrid and Theodore could not have been more excited.

Peterio says "*Although there is some radio communication between the different planets at Andromeda Galaxy and those at the Milky Way Galaxy, there really has been no major exploratory radio astronomy project here. Colonisation at the planets started in the 22nd, 23rd, 24th century AD in this galaxy. Not many observatories were built here compared to the set up throughout the planets at the Milky Way colonies. There are amateur astronomers who are using their telescopes in backyard projects and in the field, studies led by the astronomy clubs. They are carrying out small scale explorations in the studies of space nearby. It is part of the ongoing work for astronomers headquartered at Earth."*

*"How did they find these planets where the colonists have settled? "*asks Tedrid who is very curious.

"Within the last 500 years, this space in the Andromeda Galaxy had been investigated. Since the early days of space exploration! Before the colonists came, discovery and exploration were made by space telescopes. Finally, it was the teams of astronauts who landed and surveyed the planets here, who judged it safe for colonisation. It was all led by Force, who made the final evaluations on choice of planets " remarks Peterio who is certainly assured and confident about these settlements in this region of the Universe.

Andreus joins in this conversation, *" By this time Humans on Earth work closely with Force. Having been successful at the colonisation projects throughout different locations at Milky Way, the explorers were beginning to be restless to start an exploration at the Andromeda Galaxy. As some of them use to say "Those planets and stars at Milky Way Galaxy will be in a few billion years or so, joined with those at Andromeda Galaxy as they are moving towards each other. If the calculations are correct! Let's go to Andromeda, they would say. Both galaxies conjoined by a Human effort that can start this intended union! Let's do it!"*

"We will study the skies above these planets where all our Human colonists live, and you bet, we will search for other life out here too! " beams Peterio.

While relishing their drinks, the two, Peterio and Andreus reviewed the interplanetary studies and mapping project. Exciting as it was for Peterio to have discovered the planets where the Neanderthals and the Denisovans inhabited, Tedrid and his associates will now be including in the studies, the newly found planets where the Archaic Humans lived. A chronology of the human exploration, and settlement on each planet is being recorded in lengthy accounts, illustrating all interplanetary communication. There are no hidden agendas nor hostilities amongst the colonists, that would cause one planet to overwhelm a neighbour. Each planetarian has a story of his own to tell.

It was a decision left to the Committee of Planetary Anthropologists and the Committee for Planetary Exploration headed by Peterio to reach out to other planets nearby. This plan for an astronomy program to be based at Andromeda Galaxy is made in good time. The Archaic Human settlements have now been discovered and the Archaic Humans themselves, now included. They all understand how planets are settled with travellers from Earth. They realised that the power of Force was what made their lives on Denisovana and Neanderthala possible. The Archaic Humans are able to capture the essence of the historical views and also make progress on the future prospects.

Peterio remarks on how the Archaics love the interplanetary studies program and how they are included as passengers on these space flights. Evala says that recruiting the young ones for education programs could help in the work they would all do together. Evala concludes that tens to hundreds of thousands of years of evolution on Denisovana allowed for mental development in the Denisovans; and also over a half a century, Alfred was able to intellectualise the Denisovans.

Upon recapitulation of all these events, Theodore starts, innocently but hopefully, *"I am really pleased and feel optimistic that we at Neanderthala are part of his great venture!"*

Smiling, Peterio comments, *" Then you can be also an explorer for the Neanderthals. You can join in the work of astronomy which the Human colonist astronomers will teach you. That includes the basic theories and all the technical aspects of the field work. You will be able to explore the skies above. "*

Theodore claps his hands and laughs heartily and loudly.

" I feel left out at Galileo!" scorns Evala who got up out of her chair in indignation.

*"Shhh!"*Peterio quiets her with a finger over his mouth, and says *"It is our plan, Evala"*.

"The space we visited in the Triangulum Galaxy is yet unexplored by Earthlings " acknowledges Andreus. *"We want to keep this space remote. And we have plans to do exploratory work. There also may be another planet nearby*

Galileo with intelligent life."

"Well, I know of one group who fits in the category of intelligent life. It is our Galileans. The Galileans are the Homo sapiens who were making a transition to be the modern man, Homo sapiens sapiens. If left on Earth, they may have evolved over eons and distinguished from the Archaic Humans. Some Sapiens mated with the Neanderthals and the Denisovans. Some stayed isolated. The intellectual development of Homo sapiens sapiens here at Galileo, is not on an evolutionary time scale but in a historical time scale, now. We interfered. They now are adapting to us and our space age technology. You have a great project here to study human development. Early Man, and making rapid advancements in cognitive development and mental adaptations! The Human brain at that stage compared to what it is now, has never been studied." adds Peterio.

Evala points out *"On Earth, important knowledge was assembled into the brains of Humans who were not technological, and that a technological mentality was made in just over 300 years. Technological thinking took shape from the 1700's when Sir Issac Newton formed mathematical methods in the study of mechanics in physics, and it continued to the study of quantum computerization in the 2000's. It is only a dozen generations. But, as you know, these technological advances can be learned in the space of one human lifetime too. Perhaps, the brain of Modern Man may have quite a potential to develop, from a non technological stage to the one that is.   Then how far back has this mental potential been in existence. We shall see how."* smiled Evala who is now very joyful.

This meeting was loudly boisterous, made so by the debating and the happiness expressed over the new project. Before departing to their rooms to rest, they peer through the telescopes into the darkness beyond, into a night sky lit by stars throughout the night. Their planet which is their new home, has a belonging with these distant and far away stars. This space is new yet to the Human eye. Here out amongst this ceiling of sparkling newness, they laughed about their opportunity in making discoveries each night.

Meanwhile, back at Denisovana, there stirred a lot of commotion about extraterrestrial visits. The Denisovans are sharing excitedly their unusual story of visitors who landed at Denisovana when Alfred was leading the mapping project. All the different colonists who came by to Denisovana listened to these stories of extraterrestrial visits. The extraterrestrials were recorded on video and audio equipment. They resembled an altered version of the Human being;

their stature being larger in height. Dressed in space suits they could not be described visually. They communicated; and the antennas, other radio receivers and modems of computers registered all this relay of messages. However,their language could not be decoded into any understandable message. As quickly as they came, they left. The sudden departure, and the inability to make any contact communication with Alfred made their visit very questionable. All the colonists are friendly and are ready to contact with these aliens who came to visit.

Over the years, the observatories and massive telescopes with panoramic range were built on each planet. Every Colonist and Archaic Human settlement are able to explore their skies above. All incoming radio waves are received at the antennas of satellites and at radio receiver dishes located at the planets. Radio wave data are studied to build models of the activities of stars and planets. Computers make calculations and all digital data are decoded for analysis. Radio messages are also sent in order to promote contact with any intelligent life that may be able to receive such. Astronomy is now enlivened at the Galaxy Andromeda.   New data retrieved from current exploratory studies into the surrounding skyscape is now the news of the day.

The quietness of the night pervades throughout the vast terrain of the planets. But it does not dampen the local, lively talks of the astronomers who peer through the telescopes into the sky, each night. The Universe is alive with information and it is examined with the greatest sense of achievement. The planetarians now feel a sense of belonging to this vastness of space, the more they explore the skies.

On a clear sky one evening at Denisovana , both Peterio and Tedrid are out in the fields with their telescopes.Peterio remarks to Tedrid. *"On Earth, the sight of some bright stars appearing together resembled a drawing of images of animals or mythical Gods, to the early sky watchers. These star drawings are called the constellations, and can be located and viewed from all over the Earth. Can we see some new stars tonight, I wonder, and make a discovery of some new constellations, while we are here?"*

"I never had so much fun and I am proud of what I can see up in the skies" laughs Tedrid. The two stay out late as they are eager to look for pictorial images in the sky before they return to their cabins for the night.

There is a night and a day as the planets make a rotation about its axis. The stars above seem to shine and stay in their place until the astronomers, and Peterio and Tedrid return the next time. Shooting through the night skies are meteors, asteroids, rogue planets and moving stars.

Each night, sky watchers who are bubbling with excitement, made it out into the open fields to scan for flashing lights also. They could be signals of life from beyond. Unidentified flying objects are seen with curiosity and with more than the usual enthusiasm for those who are seeking extraterrestrial intelligent life in the Universe.

Flying objects do appear visibly into view, shoot by, and also disappear from the night sky.

Chapter 3   Flying Objects Identified

Unidentified flying objects became the popular talk amongst those at Denisovana. Tedrid announces in a speech that since their participation in the project of Interplanetary Radio Astronomy they may have been observed by aliens.

"Our signals " he explains to the crowd, *"were sent outward into the direction of other planets, and not to the nearby planets which are inhabited by the colonists"*.

The Denisovans send ongoing radio signals back and forth with the colonists. Beyond this communication, the astronomers in this region have also sent outwards a message to illustrate the Human identity and its presence in the Andromeda Galaxy. They were signals that gave locations where the Humans have established themselves, based on the mapping of this region of the universe.

"Could it be that we are now located and we are on the maps of these aliens? Being so, that explains why there are so many unidentified flying objects that we detect in our skies." Tedrid remarks with caution. *"They have landed here before but left in a hurry. We are friendly and if it*

Years go by and the flying objects continue to be sighted by the Denisovans and the Neanderthals. It appears oddly strange that the reports of these flying objects were mostly at the planets where these Ancient Humans live.

Busy as they were, the colonists who had reported fewer sightings, did not anticipate as seriously any landing by these foreign visitors as does the Ancient Humans.

The word spread throughout the two planets where the Ancient Humans inhabit, about the initial visit at Denisovana. If there will be further landings at their planets, then the Denisovans and the Neanderthals will be ready. They all talk about an encounter with other space farers. They remark that the Human Colonists were strangers. When Humans landed at these planets where they lived, all went well and now these Archaics are part of an interplanetary visiting program with these space faring colonists. They both are looking forward to a meeting with more space farers.

The Human colonists are more careful about visitors from other planets. But indeed, it is the work of a group of Human astronomers who actually created all the radio messages that the radio astronomers sent out into deep space. They too are looking forward to any signals coming in their direction that would give information on who responded to their signals.

In turn, there occurred a landing of alien visitors again.   This landing of the alien visitors at Neanderthala was viewed by a huge crowd of Neanderthals and a few of the Humans. On this memorable day a space craft begins to appear close to Neanderthala. All watching the skies quiet down. A smaller space vehicle departs from the larger oblong space ship which also is in view, to land at Neanderthala.The Neanderthal group gathers around the space vehicle. There was total silence when the door of the vehicle opens. Stepping out into view are two extraterrestrial aliens who give a wave to the crowd in suggestion of a friendly visit.

One of the two visitors yells out loudly, *"We are here on a friendly visit!"* This fluency in English confused the Neanderthals who spoke in both Neanderthal and in

English, that these visitors may be Human.

The extraterrestrials are smaller, being only 3 feet in height and slight in stature. Folded in their back are huge leathery wings. One expanded his wings to reveal to the Neanderthals that they are from elsewhere. These aliens are bipedal, and have a set of two arms with hands to make gestures as they talk. They can come aboard Neanderthala without their space suits. They are bare chested with hair, but the rest of their body clothed and armed with weapons and communication tools. They have boots on and a headgear. Like Humans they have eyes, but 2 are in the front, 2 on the sides and 1 in the back. They also have a broad nose and a wide mouth with teeth. They kept holding up and moving from side to side one of two hands, sometimes both. It can be seen that their hands are detecting Infrared radiation (IR), and thereby the motion of warm bodies. Such mechanism is allowing their detection of approaching beings.

"We learn English from our communication with Force. He enabled us to watch you in our minds and on communication ports on our planet. This is how we can learn your language. This is why we are here." informs the alien visitor.

"I am Theodore. We are Neanderthals. We welcome your visit. And why do you come here?" enquires Theodore.

"We are Flyers. We are here on your planet to make friends with you. We are exploring this part of the Andromeda Galaxy" answers the alien visitor.

"Welcome again" says Theordore.

"We also know of Mariners who are currently making a visit with Denisovans. They speak a little English also. They are our friends and together we are helping each other to explore this region!" reveals the alien visitor.

Thus, having made a friendly introduction, the two aliens sent back to the space ship information of the Neanderthals. Afterwards they proceed to visit with the Neanderthals. Theodore leads the two alien visitors who can walk to the village where these Neanderthals live. Theodore gives each visitor a bottle of water. He explains that they can eat their own food that they have brought along. The Neanderthals introduce these new visitors to the few Human scientists who are busy working at this planet. The Humans who are on average 6 feet in height, tower over both the Neanderthals who are shorter at 4 or 5 feet and the alien visitors. The Humans tell how Peterio, their leader will be excited about this visit. Peterio is at Denisovana with Tedrid working out the details of an astronomy project. Theodore and the Human scientists are carrying out a lively conversation and willingly describe to these strangers their astronomy project.

"Force has revealed to us who dwells in this region! This is how we got the message about your settlement here "remarks the alien visitor.

Theodore tells them,*"We have sent out under the leadership of the Human astronomers messages out to space."*

"Yes, we are located at the far edge of the Andromeda Galaxy and we may have received your messages." replies the alien visitor.

The day was spent in an introductory manner and all parties are happy about the cooperative manner in which they communicate. The extraterrestrials showed the Humans and the Neanderthals there, how they can fly around above the terrain and then settle down on different locales. They can both use their wings in flight and legs to walk or run. All those who are witness to this, express amazement and awe. Then for a challenge, one of the alien visitors invites Theodore and the Human scientists to join them for a tour of the space vehicle.

The Humans wanted Theodore to suggest a break. While the aliens can return to their space vehicle for the time out, allowing time for a discussion by the Humans with the Neanderthals. The Humans recommended that one Human and Theodore visit the space vehicle while there be a guard group outside the vehicle.

"The door must be left open and we must always be in contact and knowledgeable of what you are involved in." says Harry, a Human astronomer. *"We will just be outside and we have weapons"*.

"I understand." replies Theodore.

So, the two alien visitors lead Theodore and Simon, another Human scientist, into the space vehicle. They are shown around the inside of a circular shaped space craft which can hover above ground and accommodate up to six passengers. *"A little crowded"* is the sentiment of Simon who is so much bigger than the alien visitors. Promptly having made the visit, they come outside again, smiling.

It is agreed that this news will be made known in a jiff to the Committee of Planetary Exploration, especially to Peterio and Andreus. It was also agreed that the alien visitors should soon return to the spaceship to tell of their landing at Neanderthala and all that happened.

The very next day, the Neanderthals find the field empty of the space vehicle. The space vehicle must have left in a hurry for the space ship, which remains not far away. Quite beleaguered by all that is happening, Theodore knows what he must do. He calls up Harry and Simon about the news of the departure of the visitors from Neanderthala. They quickly send a communique to Peterio.

Upon getting this communique, Peterio thought about what is happening. He is convinced that such an occurence must be another indication that they are now in the *"times for more alien visitations"*. He is now really filled with enthusiasm and wonders if he is prepared for something brand new, like these events.

Alas, at Denisovana, Peterio, Tedrid, and Andreus were called out one day to go out to the field next to town. To everyone's surprise, they also witnessed a landing of an alien visitor. The aliens were the same ones who made a previous visit at Denisovana. That first time, Alfred had taken some instruments and recorded both audio and visual data. This second visit made an impression with those at Denisovana. They will put more effort into a communication to find out more about the visitors. The question remains why are these aliens making this second visit?

Peterio knows about this former visit, but he is more than thrilled to see them in person as they walk out of the space craft this time. But as the crowd closed in, the alien visitors started a departure for their space vehicle, to leave in a hurry again. Once more, this action seemed odd.

Peterio upon getting the news of the contact event at Neanderthala, feels need to call up an urgent meeting with all those concerned. A few days later at the Assembly Hall in Neanderthala, Peterio reminds all of the listeners, about the visits from space suited travellers at Denisovana. Whereas Theodore and Simon speak of their visitors, the Flyers at

Neanderthala and mentions that they were trusted by the Flyers as they took water from Theodore. Also, these aliens who were winged, were eager to show off their flying abilities. Simon reveals of his invitation to explore the space vehicle. In this happier note, Theodore mentions that all those at Neanderthala trust the alien visitors, in return.

What was the plan of these alien visitors? For the Humans here at Andromeda to contact with them? The Flyers know the other visitors, the Mariners who made landings at Denisovana. These questions were on everyone's mind.

Peterio has remarks about how the Mariners could not accommodate their stay at the planet Denisovana. He points out that they wore their bulky space suits throughout the entire visit. He conjectures about this observation. *"The alien visitors of Neanderthala must be accustomed to the atmospheric conditions of Neanderthala which is similar to that of Earth. Consumption of oxygen and expulsion of carbon dioxide, at temperatures and pressures here, support the life derived from Earth. It is suitable for the Flyers, too. These conditions must have been detected as they were able to abandon space suits. On the other hand, the Mariner, as their name suggests, cope in an environment that has a more humid, wetter atmosphere.*

Denisovana is Earth-like also. Confronted by hostile conditions, these aliens decide to depart when the Denisovans approach."

These particular visits surprised and worried Peterio and Andreus. In the meantime, Peterio and Andreus set up rules for actions that will be allowed and those that will be prohibited. One action to be allowed, is any friendly visitation by a space faring alien who can land on their planet. The action to be prohibited is, to partake in travels to alien planets.

Chapter 4   Safety Measures on the Agenda

There is a reaction and response from Theodore when Peterio comments on his distrust of extra-Human life. Peterio questions the aim of their visitations on planets that are settled by Earthlings. The sudden contact with the Archaic Humans at Neanderthala; has not been met with any opposition with the Neanderthals. This behaviour from the Neanderthals really prompts a nervous reaction, also from the Humans. The Human settlers who live at the outposts where these Archaics are, feel that they have more educated and sophisticated understanding of these matters.

Peterio wonders if he needs to set up a defence system here at the Andromeda colonies. This is also the attitude of all the Humans who live at Neanderthala, and at Denisovana. Surely, they must reveal to any new visitors, the message that the inhabitants be safe at all times. For now, he restricted the Neanderthals from leaving their planet on any explorative agenda, except with Humans to their own colony planets. They are prohibited from any visits with the extra-Human visitors.

Peterio in the next few weeks, departs for his long journey back to Earth for peer advice. He ponders over the required secret protocol in making this arrangement. He must get through a system of secret coded passages. He will be arranging a secret ad hoc meeting with military defence leaders. All this planning is kept alive only in Peterio's mind, as he never leaks to anyone his schedule.

At the administration headquarters for the Earth Space Agency, Peterio passes through his first step. At a desk with a computer terminal, he speaks to the computer, providing passwords and all required personal information. Meanwhile, he places on his head, a helmut. This special helmut is constructed for communication with the computer through the mind. Peterio sends out a coded message, by thinking out a sentence. *"A thousand cats roamed and one sat by."* He coded the number 1001, for the receivers to pick up. He coded the number "1000" for emergency and the number "1" as he is the only one on the mission for now. He gets his message through, to the receivers at the other end of the relay. He has made contact with some human administrator. Suddenly, a voice speaks to Peterio inside his helmut. The planet name is flashed into his head, *"Minerva"*. He understands what that means. The meeting location will be at the planet, Minerva, at a nearby solar system in the Milky Way.

Peterio knows what to do. He must travel to Minerva. At the Minerva Space Agency Administration Building, he will find out where to meet with leaders. Again, this will be done ad hoc. He is ready to mobilize anytime. Peterio arrives at the computer terminal at Minerva and the message is again communicated through the helmet. He heard. *"Cut trees until the timberline is reached"*. Peterio knows now where the meeting will be. It coded for the military outpost that is established at the edge of a surrounding forest, in Minerva.

Peterio gets going, not leaving a trace of the secret that he is about to discuss, at the Minerva Space Agency. He sets afoot to that outpost.

At the meeting, Peterio talks about space defence, with his peers who came from all over the Milky Way. There are several military leaders from Earth. On the agenda is the plan for the development of a time-warp, space defence system. Defence missiles and artillery, along with the soldiers of the defence department can, in this scheme be deployed from Earth in a warp speed, space pathway.   By teleportation they can be transported from the bases at the Milky Way Galaxy to the colonies at the Andromeda Galaxy.

The Andromeda colonies at present have no military space defence weaponry or bases to defend itself. This is the time henceforth, to protect the colonies at the Andromeda Galaxy. Safety for the colonists is the utmost of importance!

Chapter 5   What? A Rebellion

As Peterio sets off for this mission to seek some space defence for the Andromeda colonies, in the meanwhile, the Flyers return to Neanderthala for another visit. The Flyers put into action what Peterio predicted was going to occur. The Flyers befriend Theodore and during this contact meeting, they offer Theodore a ride with them back to their planet far away. Encouraged, Theodore makes an announcement at the Assembly Hall to the Neanderthals and Humans there. The Neanderthals are all in agreement and supported this promising idea.

This attitude of the Neanderthals alarmed the Humans at Neanderthala. Simon was alerted by Harry. Together they discuss these ideas assumed by the Neanderthals. According to the order received from Peterio, restriction on outer space visits beyond the Human colonies are to be enforced. Harry and Simon decide to hold a meeting with Theodore. For every day the Flyers are aboard Neanderthala, these two and other Humans feel the pressure that was on them to uphold the orders from Peterio. The Humans must impart to the Neanderthals a sense for loyalty to the cause of the Humans, their relatives, and not to alien visitors, the strangers.

Simon asks Theodore, " *Why are you resisting us? You must not go and oppose our rules.*"

"*But I am a friend now with the Flyers.*" Theodore remarks in reaction to the comment by Simon.

"*We are of the same Human family, the Homo genus from Earth. We must co-operate together!*" responds Simon.

Theodore rebukes, "*We met you, Homo sapiens, and befriended you. We trusted you and explored the regions here in outer space travels. But it is a kind offer, that our new friend, the Flyers made, to allow me to travel and visit their planet. It is no different from those offers I took, when I made visits with the Human colonies here. I see no problem in this action.*"

Simon knows what these words from Theodore mean. The next day, when the Neanderthals go to the field to see the Flyers, they are astonished by what they see. The Humans are banded together to form a Human blockade. They all made arm links by looping their arms together. They are standing in front of the space vehicle preventing further contact of these Neanderthals with the Flyers. It comes down to a push and a shove. The Neanderthals now are angered for the confrontation they are having with their Human relatives.

Suddenly, the space vehicle shoots for the skies and disappears. As the Flyers leave, the Neanderthals become very sad and disappointed. Short of a fight with the Humans in the field at present, they all go home. They will avoid the obvious action to take, that is to start a rebellion. Harry and Simon now think that a real confrontation with the Neanderthals may arise. The mistrust amongst all filled the air, and the contentment that was there earlier has disappeared.

"Let us talk with them again! It will be easier as the Flyers have left. We do not want a rebellion." reassures Simon.

As the Flyers are not at Neanderthala, there is a sentiment of antagonistic resentment from the Neanderthals towards the Humans. There is little opportunity for any activity which the Neanderthals can do with the Humans together, now. Avoidance with each other replaced their usual get-together. What the Humans and Neanderthals are giving to each other, is the silent treatment. While the Flyers are not present, the quietness in this colony was maintained. Simon and Harry did their best to prevent outbreak of anger or fighting.

Meanwhile, the defence plans for the Andromeda Galaxy are held top secret. The plans are only to be sent to the planetary leaders of the Andromeda Galaxy, in secret communiques. The communiques for space defence are initiating widespread worries and prompting discussion amongst the leaders. As they are also alerted of the frequent visits by extra-Human visitors at Neanderthala, pressure to obtain security becomes more immediate.

Peterio's wife, Lauren who is also one of the leaders, disagrees with the plan for a space defence system. Lauren is a social biologist who studies the inhabitants at the Andromeda colonies. She has studied on Earth where she was born. She works with Evala at Galileo, Triangulum Galaxy, presently. Evala builds research data in genetics from her studies on Early Homo sapiens, who are current inhabitants of Galileo. Together Evala and Lauren coordinate lots of data for the research into Human evolution and development at both the Triangulum Galaxy and the Andromeda

Galaxy. They also get feedback from Gisellin's work with super-computers on genes.

Lauren decides on a tactic to intercept the defence plan. She must go to Earth and then to Minerva. Her mission, to make a plea for the planets at Andromeda Galaxy to remain unarmed, is solely currently, her own effort.

At the meeting in Minerva, with the defence department leaders and Peterio, Lauren expresses her opinion of the 400-year history of the colonists at the Andromeda Galaxy.

"With peaceful manners, the Human colonists survive at the Andromeda Galaxy!" explains Lauren.

Lauren may be turning the heads of the defence leaders. Lauren states *"The visitors and UFOs neither endanger the planets nor its inhabitants. These are intelligent and friendly visitors who do not exhibit aggression at these planets. The alien visitors appear to be careful. We must be careful also!"*Lauren remarks.

Everyone is in awe as Lauren makes this outrageous suggestion at their defence meeting. To all, it is even a bigger surprise when Force makes his appearance at the plea session.

Force states, "*Peaceful manners and manoeuvres will be respected. I will support and help those who work within methods that offer peaceful communication.*" Force claims, "*I will not teleport artillery nor soldiers for warfare, to the Andromeda Galaxy colonies*".

All were immobilised in their waiting for a reaction to the comments made by Force. Shocked by the words spoke by Force, most sit in silence.

Force goes on to say, "This system for defence was initiated in the Milky Way to protect Earth from aliens. To date, although the system was an accommodating one, no event put this defence system at Earth or beyond to the test. There never were any invasions by Extra-Terrestrials at the Milky Way colonies."

"*You are right that there were no invasions. But, as early as the 20th Century AD, we on Earth have sighted UFOs in our skies. There were speculations of landings.*" says the Military leader, General Oliver.

Peterio responds, " *Lots of information had surfaced to reveal that these UFOs may have travelled from a future time."*

''Well, the situation, on hand is more than real for us now. We cannot speculate on anything. They are at Andromeda at our colonies." quipped the General.

"Maybe, they are at the Andromeda Galaxy. But it is 2500 AD. And they may continue to travel to visit the Milky Way in its future. Then what if they travel from this future to visit Earth in its past. We could have witnessed them as the UFOs that were sighted long ago." ponders Peterio.

"So, they can travel far away.   Long distance travel and time travel is in their command. Is that what you're saying Peterio?" asked the General.

"Yes, I think that they are intelligent and capable like us! " stated Peterio.

"And they seem to appear as Ambassadors of Peace. They are friendly. They have harmed no one." adds Lauren.

Force speaks again. *" I do not want to restrict these visitors. They are friendly!"*

There follows a debate over the next days, to re-evaluate the final decisions. The meeting of the defence leaders with Peterio, Lauren and the Force gives way to become respectful of extraterrestrial visitations. Alas, the rejection of the plan to deploy by the teleport method, weapons or soldiers to the Andromeda Galaxy is enacted. The military space defence system intended for this Galaxy is now negated.

Peterio looks forward to, anticipating for what Force states and intends concerning peaceful methods of communication. He thinks about Force and His intricate knowledge of His Universe!

Chapter 6   Excitement Over UFO

Back home at Andromeda, Peterio delivers his message to the Neanderthals and Humans at Neanderthala and those at Denisanova. The good news was the abandonment by the military leaders, of the plans to build a deployable military defence system which can be sent to Andromeda from Earth. It would have needed Force and a teleportation system that Force would arrange. In retrospect, the Humans at these two planets consider whether the defence system can bring security and safety.

There is much abuzz amongst the inhabitants everywhere, about this controversial issue. There is at present no artillery nor sophisticated military bases here. These Human colonies are like any pioneer one focused on scientific ideas of exploration and discovery. Similar in mission but with the exception that they are much more technologically advanced and civilised with 26th Century sophistication. Unlike the stories from 20th Century science fiction which projected the stories of space age wars, these settlements are mainly concerned about their lifestyles and goals at these planets and not on space wars with aliens. In fact, there are no alien visits till now. Although such topics surfaced in their talks, these settlers cannot fathom the idea of warfare with any alien visitor.

Could the Force know more than, they can imagine about why all these security measures are not necessary. That is also being pursued with much discussion. But somehow, they feel safe and will continue to put their trust in the Force.

Peterio is delighted that his wife Lauren came forward on these ideas. In their brief visit to Denisovana, they have been both in agreement over a difficult question. They quickly move from this topic of defence to discuss at length the exciting topic of the UFOs and visits by friendly aliens.

Peterio smilingly announces to Lauren, " *We have reached the next stage in our plans to live far away from Earth.*"

Lauren replies and laughingly says "*This time that we are sharing with all the others is very exciting and important. To find intelligent non-Human life has been our main goal also.*"

"This is really very surprising but we welcome it. These extraterrestrials came to find us. And we are all here!" adds Peterio.

*"You have talked to and raised our children on these ideas!" You must tell them! "*demands Lauren.

Peterio exclaims *" We have a dozen generations of our descendants. I will send out communiques to all of them! No! Better than that. I will go find each and everyone and bring them back to Denisovana or Neanderthala. Each will stay here and be a witness for himself. It will be an experience that each will cherish. "*

"I can join you for that!"   Lauren says in reaction.

"This is the most beautiful time in our lives" Peterio says, then kisses and embraces his wife and together they go off in their joyous union.

Months later, the conference on UFO takes place. It is at the headquarters at Denisovana where Tedrid is leader of the Mapping and Chronology of Interplanetary Voyages Project. Everyone at the conference is buzzing about UFOs in the skies of their planets. They talk about how the two visits of aliens at Denisovana was very mysterious and the one at

Neanderthala was informative and friendly. They conclude that the Humans and Archaic Humans were welcoming. Perhaps, as someone suggests, that the differences in the visits had to do with differences in the two visitors.

Theodore tells the conference goers *"These visitors appear to be highly intelligent. They left before any confrontation can happen. They learned the English language!"*

Simon remarks *"They were in communication with the Force. Certainly, they knew of us before they came. They travel to other planets, especially to ones where there is life on it. "*

"And indeed, they came here before our radioastronomy messages were received by them." points out Peterio.

Tedrid reflects on the UFOs. *"There is a lot of UFOs in the skies. Who are all these visitors? And they just fly over. No landing. What planets are they travelling from? And why?"*

Peterio tackles this question. *" Theodore suggests the visitors, the Flyers are friendly and left a lot of information with us. They seem to know the visitors to Denisovana. I wonder if there are others who have travelled here with these two species. Could their expeditions just be exploration? Or could there be other reasons to involve us?"*

Force having listened in on all the comments on UFOs and the alien visitors, will now speak out. *"I am very delighted for all your very enthusiastic interests on alien visitors. To me they are not alien. I have known these travellers since ages ago. They are sophisticated and intelligent. They did not need me to help them in their interstellar voyages. Their visits here were agreeable to me and to be commended for their eagerness to make friends. They are from far, far away. "*

Peterio speaks with Force on this important matter. *"We feel good now about the whole visit because you know about our visitation with aliens and about the visitors, themselves. We are eager to visit them. If they live far, far away, we will work with you Force, on teleportation and the warp speed voyage."*

Force reveals *"There are other planets here, in this vicinity, inhabited by different kinds of life forms. I want you to continue to explore this region and document your visits. I am happy about the radio astronomy project, in its outward missions to reach further beyond, for studies on this Andromeda Galaxy and for possible signs of intelligent life. I am pleased that you are hopeful to make new discoveries. I know that Peterio's Committee on Interplanetary Voyages is also making progress. But if, you also want, I can set up a special search for intelligent life further beyond. This I did for your visitors!"*

Everyone cannot be more overjoyed. They really feel for their exploratory mission-oriented life out here far away from Earth.

Chapter 7   On a New Path

Andreus arrives at Galileo, Triangulum Galaxy. This visit, many years removed from when he and Peterio first arrived here is like arriving home to familiar grounds.

When Peterio and Andreus first set foot on Galileo, they noticed that it was only inhabited by a small tribe of primitive people and some wild animals. These people were scattered about in small groups throughout the landscape of plains and tree-filled fields. Peterio and Andreus made a friendly introduction with these primitives after they were assured that there will be no conflict. These primitives recognised that Peterio and Andreus came from the skies and were different from what they could understand. They were fascinated by the space vehicle and some equipment that the two visitors had brought along. Letting their fascination suppress any reserve on their part, they started friendly communications with these two strangers. These early people turned out to be early Homo sapiens as indicated by blood tests that Evala performed.

It was an illuminating experience when at a conference on Earth, many years after Peterio's contact, the Force announced that He transferred them there, long ago. They are now at a planet, in which Peterio as a Space Age traveller in the 26th Century AD, can visit. They are still the primitive early Man. Force arranged a time warp teleportation to the planet for these primitive Homo sapiens. In this setting, the Primitive meets with Space Age. Their advancement on Earth had just brought them to work with fire and build a shelter. They may have advanced a little on Galileo, when they were discovered by Peterio. From visits to Andromeda over the years, Peterio and Andreus brought back technology to help train their advancement.

Andreus has a work order to tackle how the development of this population of Early Man were to take place. He must meet with Evala and plan with her firstly. Evala had been working on the genetics of this population of Homo sapiens. As the Force had alluded, this population of Homo sapiens had not previously mated with Homo neanderthalensis nor with the Homo denisovans. As with the Neanderthals at Neanderthala, and the Denisovans at Denisovana they have been taken from populations on Earth that have not intermingled yet either.

Andreus and Evala recaptured their ideas on this. Evala starts off, in a happy observation. *"There was intermarriage amongst the different species of Archaic Humans on Earth. Maybe it has to do with their survival tactics because eventually, the Neanderthals and Denisovans went extinct. Or maybe they were mostly transported here. Do you know the answer?"*

Andreus scratched his head indicating that this was a question he cannot answer. *"I wish I knew all that happened, so I can figure out what the purpose of these Archaic colonies were meant to be. The Neanderthals are advancing on their own initiatives and with us very fast as did the Denisovans. They may have had a longer time on their own planets to evolve and develop. The Force talked at the conference on Earth that he wanted the different subspecies of the Homo genus to meet in a Space Age setting. Maybe, it was a chance to put each of these species on its own planets to watch for a different course in the evolution of this genus."*

Evala questions *"But are we allowing that? We are training them on technology?"*

Andreus says *"It could be about the times. The Primitive*

and the Space Age? In the sense that they can develop quickly to the Space Age and avoid the different routes that blocked mankind."

Evala commented on that. *"There were masses of peoples in different countries that need to be taken care of. Throughout history, different routes were used to govern the peoples.   But different governments never agreed on different ways to live. There were much, too much hostility and warfare on Earth. Even in the 20th Century after World Wars, there were still much war-driven ideas on the Earth."*

"Perhaps, Force stepped in to populate these planets so that these other subspecies can still exist to date. Separation onto their own planets allowed them a place in the future. The fights for survival may have caused hostile approaches in the Human evolutionary makeup long ago." points out Andreus.

Evala agrees *"Like in the days, 50,000 years ago, when survival in threatening circumstances meant for these primitives to do whatever they could do to survive. Maybe the ones who got together and intermarried, worked on survival together. Those others perished. "*

"Force explained that He took the Primitive Men long ago

before that." reminds Andreus.

Evala says happily again, *"It really is about us. We, the Space Age meet up with the Primitives. We can study development and evolution of Primitive Man"*

Andreus thinks and states, *"The Primitives are very pacifist-oriented. Especially now that we are here to help them. Do you know also, that over the centuries the Space Age colonies of Homo sapiens here at Andromeda are very much oriented to co-operation. So far away from everyone else, that's what I surmise"*

Evala agrees to study carefully. *"All Early Man on Earth were together at first and the differences caused hostility to nurture. I will study social and physical development in all these Primitives now. They are here alone on the planets except for us whom they appreciate. This will be a different course of study in Evo-Devo."*

Andreus loves to talk about this and he will be here to help Evala. They conclude that a new Evo-Devo will be taking place at Galileo, Triangulum Galaxy for the Early Humans. What will be its outcome? For the Neanderthals and the Denisovans, their lives have changed already.

Chapter 8   Force

Force is the universal guardian of life.   He has knowledge of all the planets and their locations in the Universe. He has sole knowledge of all the life that are inhabitants of the planets. He alone has a panoramic insight of what life means.   Moreover, he has introduced himself to all intelligent life forms.   He speaks to the different life all over in unique ways that make communication possible. When possibly necessary, he has arranged for communication contacts between various life forms from different planets.

Force has within His reach the element of time. He can arrange time-warps for travellers to travel to and from the future or the past.   He can organise teleportation to short distances, and also in rapid warp-speed to far away places. He has arranged for some of His travelling crew like Peterio to administer and arrange their own control of the teleport on their spaceships and space vehicles.

Force is a power.   Force is an entity or a form grandiose.   Force has saved many a life form from harm. Also, He has demonstrated that He can send other life to carry out the task to save. Moreover, He has demonstrated that He will follow the course of natural processes in the Universe, although He has the power and supernatural abilities to control. In this way He allows for the natural, physical processes of the Universe to carry forth. The Force works with the Universe and finds it beautiful ever present.

Peterio is one of Force's crew of time travellers. Peterio, who like all his other colleagues who time and space travel, has longevity in his life. Peterio is 550 years old. Peterio has ability to cooperate and is a loyal follower of Force. He has ability to carry out the missions for Force. He often wonders what Force will set up, next for him to do. Peterio being a very capable person and can adapt to difficult situations, finds the missions challenging but rewarding. He has been blindly led to help the Neanderthal populations in numerous, troubling times; and he did more than accomplish the tasks at hand, to save them. He by now, has paved the way for the Human colonists to make friends with his Archaic Human group.

Peterio is more than excited for his own future. The Force has made the announcement that travelling with

Him to visit other life forms is now an agenda item for these very enthusiastic travellers. Peterio has a goal like those other colleagues. These colonists had made their way to live in outer space conditions. Time and space travelling is more than just their work. It was their dream and wish as they set out from Earth. It is an ideology different from those who did not want to pursue outer space life. They are explorers and to make a discovery in space expeditions is now second nature. The Universe has diversity of life! Out here each can possibly encounter foreign life.

Peterio ponders over what Force said. Force has lots of information that He keeps to himself. Peterio knows He will guide him to the next encounter and He must trust the Force. He wonders if this next encounter will be to the two visitors that landed on Neanderthala and Denisovana. These visitors were secretive, themselves about how much and what information, they would deliver to the Human crowd. He remembers that they had communicated with Force before they came for the visit. He can now see clearly about what these visitors were about. All who saw them had realised that they were intelligent and friendly. The very situation may have been planned in this manner, to be little bit elusive and hard to understand. But having heard from the Force, Peterio now feels good about it all. He and his peers changed their minds on the military defence system and he is really glad for that, now.

In the months that follow, Peterio co-ordinates his thoughts. He has reached out to all his family members and they are also very grateful for all that is happening. Peterio is moving into another stage of his life. He has more insight than the others in space travel now. He believes the Force is a teacher and he will be learning about the Force's Universe.

Peterio reaches out to Force about their next trip to visit extra Human life. The Force in this conversation declares that the visitors are very intelligent. He says that these visitors are highly sophisticated beings who would be of interests to Peterio, but they live far, far away. He tells Peterio that He had worked with them in the recent past. But He says He will not take Peterio to where they are. Instead, He is sure that Peterio will be delighted to see other life that He knows of. Force wants Peterio to appreciate what he is going to see. He tells Peterio that these life forms live nearby the Human colonies in the Andromeda Galaxy, and that Peterio will see and be rewarded by this voyage of discovery.

Peterio delivers this message to his colleague, Andreus who is still in Galileo, and to his wife, Lauren who is with him, presently. They will be part of the Human crew in this brand new challenge. Andreus writes back that definitely he wants to communicate with life other than Earth derived Humans. He also, like the others want to learn much about life in other parts of the Universe and how it may evolve. He will take a break from his work with Evala to join in with this travelling crew.

So, the news about Force and the crew of this expedition reached all the colonists everywhere at Andromeda Galaxy, Triangulum Galaxy and those at Milky Way Galaxy. The Earth is proud of their heroic space travellers. Earthlings have achieved much and now they are reaching out to be team-mates with the Force.

Chapter 9   On Board to Discover

The crew is on board the spaceship. This spaceship is one of the smaller ones of the fleet. It has in it a small space vehicle. Peterio is standing and moving around to talk to the crew in the engine-computer room. Joining him in making these greetings is Andreus. Lauren is here too, with Simon and Harry two astronomers who are taking leave from Neanderthala. Some of the Archaic Humans were allowed to participate.   On this discovery trip, Tedrid, the Denisovan and Theodore, the Neanderthal are included.

"Their opinions!" considers Peterio. *"Will be invaluable."*

The Humans has all been exposed to and has met up with lots of diverse life forms.   Back home on Earth, they kept pets and became stewards of other wildlife. They have been educated and learned about the evolution and the ecological relationships of other species. Neither Theodore nor Tedrid who was educated by Alfred Mendel were taught biology or natural history to any extent. Having been exposed to the Humans, these two now are not only eager to make explorations to far away planets and make contact friendships, but will find this trip, enlightening and educational.

Force arrives and everyone stands and clap. Force is happy and proud, and declares, *"We are ready for our big adventure! I will give some orders to the computer . "*

Within a few days, they were there. Peterio takes the others down to the surface of a very blue colored planet. He notices that the planet has some islands amongst a very watery world. They look all around the island which is mostly rocky. Some sandy beaches are hit by water slapping on the shoreline.

Andreus shouts, *"Oh my! There's a creature washed ashore. Let's go and examine."*

Peterio, Lauren and the others all start running with Andreus towards the creature.

The creature came out of the water and is now tumbling on the shore. It is globular shaped and has on its surface, some round sensors that can initiate chemotaxis. It is tumbling on its six legs which have claws at each end.

Lauren laughs because it is not threatening them as it

does not see. But using its legs, it makes a somersault motion on the shore.

Peterio states, *"It is a primitive form of life. Let's stay here and see if there are other types and forms. These creatures must be all water bound. There's not much on the island itself. That's from what I can see on the way here from the spaceship."*

Andreus takes off on his own with Theodore, towards the rocky hill to see what they can find. Then Theodore runs in another direction and calls out to Andreus to follow him.

Andreus stops running to look at some curious shapes at his feet.

"Are these plates alive?" asks Andreus. They wait to see.

Suddenly it spit out some water and air, through the hole on its topside. It is formed of concentric plates which started to expand upwards. Looking like a cone, it is sucking in air from the hole and excreting air from its base. Somehow it hovers around. Slowly but moving.

Andreus tells Theodore to take out his equipment that he carried with him, and ask the computer to take a snapshot. They will later look at what they got here. They have never been witness to something so strange. They will ask the computer if it has knowledge of anything like these life forms.

"Turn around Theodore and look here, see what's coming!" shouts Andreus as he continues his explorations.

"It's coming on to the rocks. It looks like the other one that was washed ashore!   But it has an eye looking upwards. It has a slit opening to take in water" and is walking on its legs." says Andreus. *"Notice it is making leaps and hops by expelling the water.   "It doesn't look like it belongs on the rocks. Like the other one, it is waterborne, but it can move around on shore."*

Peterio and all the crew examine the wildlife here till dark. They all go back to the space vehicle to head back to the spaceship. When these explorers got back, Force who was proud of them speaks to give some advice. He asks that all who kept notes or stored data into the computer, to give a debate on their new discoveries.

Their debate concentrated on the fact that these life forms were not like anything they've seen on Earth. They're water bound but can also get around on shore. They conclude however that none of these life forms seem to be intelligent but were primitive.

*"Maybe it has a nervous system or is it just chemotactic. There must be some systems in the globular shaped creatures. To allow it to catch food in order to grow. Does it have consciousness and maintain an awareness of its surroundings?"*questions Andreus.

Peterio reminds them that it may have a central nervous system like some kind of brain. *"Force told me that I cannot kill any to take a specimen back here. So, I am going to look for a deceased one on shore. Maybe collect some samples. We haven't gotten near the water yet."*

Peterio needs time. Force agrees that they will stay on this planet to explore further, for several months indeed.

Force implores his crew to work hard and not be afraid to go into the water. He suggests *"You will be astonished at how vast these waters are, in the way that they are inhabited by a variety of creatures who make up this water world."*

The crew that came onto this watery world are astonished at themselves. They did not think there was much to see on this desolate looking water world, at first. Using their aquatic equipment and portable transport boats, they went to explore deep beneath the surface of the oceans. The oceans are alive with unusual life. Most of the life, they notice are in forms of radial symmetry. Some are sessile attached to rocks. Some use a propelling movement, to swim. As it takes in seawater from the slits in the body, an expulsion or a blast of water through the base of its tubular body, makes it possible to swim. With flashlights on the headgear and armbands, to help shed light, it was still blurry for Peterio to see much. Peterio takes back a water sample.

Next, Peterio and Andreus decide to take a look around the waters close to the islands. They are not in the deep part of the ocean now; but on the reefs of the islands. Exploring further within the waters that are 10 meters deep of the surface, Andreus is cheerful looking around at his colourful surroundings. On the rocks were irregular or polygonal shaped forms. What Andreus notices is their colour schemes; which stretches the rainbow spectrum from purple to bluish, from green to yellowish, and orange to reddish colours. Peterio who is nearby chases after the mobile forms which are propelling their bodies throughout the waters. They do not stop to ingest any smaller forms. They are also colourful to look at, being of purplish hue. Suddenly, a round form with six legs tumbles onto and bumps into Peterio. Having done this, it bounces off him. It exhibits no fear of the two strangers in their waters. Big ones and little ones. tubular shaped, and round shaped. There is an abundance of bright color organisms, swimming or tumbling in the waters. This sunlit aquamarine site entices the two Humans to stay swimming there a little longer.

Peterio brings back a lot of pictures and water samples. Carefully he carries back some live samples to examine. These live specimens are quickly released soon after experimental protocols. Andreus concludes, "*These organisms are photosynthetic using their colourful, pigmented cells to make energy and food. They are not ingesting each other, but are autotrophic.*"

Peterio and his crew record all the data. They genuinely feel like natural history biologists on a successful discovery expedition. They all agree that it was lots of fun and a break from their usual type of voyage.

Chapter 10   More Expeditions and Voyages

All the travellers are eager and anticipating where Force will take them next.   They all tell Force that they wanted to visit with intelligent species. They want to try out different methods of communication and make contact with their alien species.   But now they also want to study those that are the primitive forms. Those in the *"budding stage of evolution"*.   They want now to learn how other forms of life exist.

They debate until they landed on their next planet. They are now going to venture on a green colour planet.

*"Is it moss that covers the rocks? "*queries these crew members as they step onto the evergreen covered rocks.

Some vertical structures are in place scattered amongst the green cover. They are nothing like the trees or shrubs on Earth.   These small vertical assemblages appear to be held to the ground by holdfast rootlets.

Peterio and Andreus use their magnifiers to take a closer look at the green structures. These green entities appeared as a unit made up of a multitude of smaller subunits. The smaller units are not made of cells. They are little plates that were bigger than cells and were leathery and tough.

"Photosynthetic entities" assumes Peterio.

"At least they won't be hungry.   They won't gobble us up!" laughs Andreus.

Some of the multi-unit entities are large and spread over the rocks. Some of the smaller masses are able to move!   They manipulate spicules located on the side next to the ground to travel slowly across the terrain. They seem to possess chemotactic and tactile perceptions. They move away from large jagged rock formations.

Andreus follows one as it moves and tests its sense or awareness. He touches it with his boot. He smiles as it inched away. He figures it must get its nutrients from the air, rain and the soil. *"Harmless creature"* he thought. There seems to be a lot of them all over. *"No predator"* he presumes.

Force wants to show the crew, a very early development form from the evolutionary scale. Force wants Peterio to study this form.

*"But it will take millions of years for any substantial evolution to occur in this life form."*notes Peterio.

"You can teleport into the future for this study" beams Force.

Andreus joins in. *"I love the study of evolution. I can go too?"*

"Yes, I can set up another crew, when this expedition is finished!" Force promises.

Everyone who ventured out to this planet, is cheering and clapping, making a lot of noise in this quiet world.

"It is a green terrestrial ecosystem here, but there must be a water basin closeby, as it circulates some rain here. There must be an aquatic ecosystem here somewhere!" ponders Andreus. He is reflecting on how this biosphere must work.

When they have all collected their data, they go back

by the space vehicle to the space-ship.   Peterio and others talk all the way back about teleportation. They all conclude that Peterio has the most experience time travelling. They will follow Peterio and Force who will guide them. They all are happy.   They can have both, time travel to the future and the opportunity to study this planet, which is inhabited by creatures based on a simple life plan.

This planet is very unusual as it is so primitive, the crew members thought. Because they will be allowed to go to its future; they will be eager to look for, the green life forms to develop and adapt to changes over time.

Peterio and Andreus compares these organisms on this planet to those of the previously visited planet. The other planet is a water world. Peterio and Andreus conjectures that life there began in the waters.

*"Those sea organisms are self sufficient autotrophs who are really not like anything on Earth! "*Peterio comments to Andreus.

Andreus laughs and thinks aloud.   *"Octopus and jellyfish!   There are ones that look like jellyfish. On Earth jellyfish are animals and heterotrophic."*   Andreus starts by saying, *"What is interesting here is that although some forms are stationary, I was impressed with the mobile ones. Their evolution on the water and on the land is interesting."*

"These ones here on this green planet are land borne autotrophs. And some have mobility! Our visits to the future of this species will tell us a lot about mobile autotrophs!" beams Peterio heartily.

This overwhelmingly exciting debate tired each and everyone out. Everyone refreshes and nourishes himself, when back at the spaceship. They all meet up again in the big lounge-conference room where they will talk to Force.

"Our last destination before this expedition is over, will be to visit the planet, where I sent you to before, Peterio. I will show you on the computer console."   Force says as He took charge.

"Oh my! It's my study of the primitive beings who have four eyes and sturdy legs to climb trees. Their planet is much like Earth. I have lots of data on them. They are nomadic. I found groups of them everywhere. Some were fishing in the water holes. Some were found in the caves taking shelter and hiding from danger. They learned to

hunt and cook over fire. But they only have a primitive communication. They have no records of any kind yet!" Peterio remembers.

"Can you attempt to communicate more with them?" asks Force.

Both Theodore and Tedrid listen intensely.

Peterio explains *"I told everyone that I attempted to communicate without all the technological gadgets and intellectual stuff I had with me. They may be similar to pre-Early Man!"*

"I want you to work with them and find out, Peterio. You have been studying them for hundreds of years. Your influence with them will help them move forward". Force agrees that Peterio is the right person for the job.

"I will take along some of my Archaic Human crew to help me out! " chuckles Peterio.

Theodore offers to help out and along with some others is ready to join in.

"Fantastic!" booms out the voice of Peterio.

They again peer into the computer console and look at the images. They all laugh. They will all communicate with these unsophisticated, uncivilised looking beings. A few days lapse and they head out for this planet.

"Let's get ready for your landing" says computer as it stations above the Earth-like planet which does not appear too foreign.

Peterio and his crew goes to the space vehicle to make the landing. He feels appreciation for his colleague, Evala who is studying Early Homo sapiens, at Galileo. *"She has an easier task,"* he feels. *"The Early Homo sapiens will evolve to be Space Age Homo sapiens, one day. To be like ourselves or more. What will these primitive beings evolve to be like?"*

Peterio reflects on his current expedition. It will be a brand new and novel study. He has much gratitude for the choices that Force made.

In this expedition, Peterio decides to entice the inhabitants of the planets with gifts of food. They will catch fish and collect berries for their new acquaintances. In return for this offer of friendship, Peterio says " *I hope the inhabitants of this planet will let myself and the crew to stay around to watch them. We will listen for their abilities to communicate."*

Peterio takes a deep breath and continues on his idea. *"Try to communicate in our language, English along with a lot of sign language, first. That way we can all understand! We will listen for their communication words and phrases. Even try telepathy! We can communicate if we are friendly! Let's go. We are here for a few months before we talk to Force."* concludes Peterio.

With this new ambitious plan, Peterio, Andreus, Lauren, Theodore and Tedrid set off on a new task. They are leading a small crew with equipment and computers.

Peterio does not get to meet those intellectually advanced visitors to Neanderthala or Denisovana on this expedition. But what a fun experience he is having on this adventure and trek of discovery!

The End

Peterio's Sketch # 1

Semi Advanced Creatures

Radial symmetry
Autotrophs
Water Borne
Land Rovers

<h1 style="text-align:center">Peterio's Sketch # 2</h1>

<h2 style="text-align:center">Early Stage Creatures</h2>

Irregular shaped
Photosynthetic Autotrophs
Landborne
Sessile or Mobile

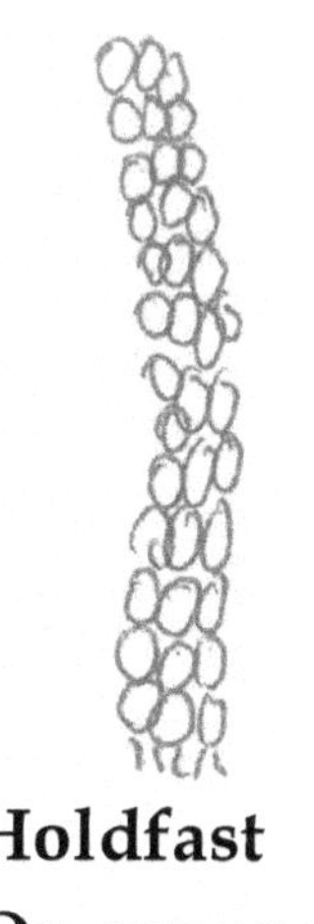

Holdfast
On ground

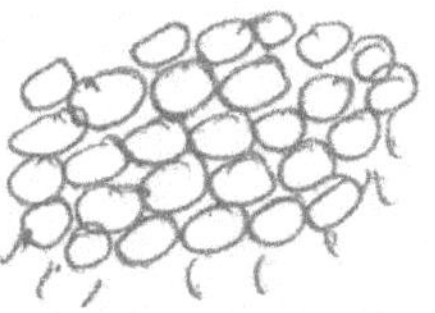

Travelling
on ground

Advanced Creatures

Landborne
Able to Climb, Walk, Run
Like Pre-Early Man
Heterotrophs

References and Further Reading

Devorkin, D & Smith, RW (2008). Imaging Space and Time Hubble, Smithsonian National Air and Space Museum in Association with National Geographic Society

Dorling Kindersley Limited, (2010). DK Featuring New Images from NASA from Earth to the Edge of the Universe, DK Publishing, New York, NY, USA

Greenstein, G. (2013). Understanding the Universe. Cambridge University Press, New York, NY. USA

Interbreeding between Archaic and Modern Humans-Wikipedia

Kerrod, R. (2005). The Star Guide. John Wiley & Sons Inc. Hoboken, New Jersey, USA.

Lee, Jean Pi, (2020).PeterioIgnitus Planetary Anthropologist. Ingramspark Inc. Tennessee, USA.

Sykes, RW. (2020). Kindred, Neanderthal LIfe, Love, Death and Art. Bloomsbury Sigma. New York,

NY.USA

Trefil, James; (2012). National Geographic Space Atlas Mapping the Universe and Beyond. Washington, D.C., USA.

Weiler, Edward J. (2010). Hubble a Journey Through Space and Time. HN Abrams Inc. In collaboration with NASA . New York, NY, USA